EGMONT
We bring stories to life

First published in Great Britain 2011 by Egmont UK Limited
239 Kensington High Street, London W8 6SA

Text copyright © Portobello Rights Limited 2011
Illustrations © Portobello Rights Limited and the BBC 2011,
taken from the BBC series 'World of Happy by Giles Andreae'
based on original illustrations by Janet Cronin

Giles Andreae has asserted his moral rights

A CIP catalogue record for this title is available from the British Library

ISBN 978 1 4052 5849 4
1 3 5 7 9 10 8 6 4 2
Printed in Italy

a story about
LOVE and HAPPINESS

my name is ....

and some of the people I love are

....

There was a time when whales were . . .

rather small.

But, long ago, there were two whales who CHANGED their kind for good.

yoo-hoo!

"I LOVE you," said the gentleman. "I do."

"I DOUBLE DIDDY love you,

Now something ODD began to happen.

At every declaration of desire,
each whale became a little
BIGGER than before.

yum!

"I TRIPLE diddy love you times a million . . . and a HALF,"

"Hmmm," the man then hmmmed.
This was not an EASY one to beat.

So he swam up to his lady
and he KISSED her.

"You great big

whale of LOVELINESS," he said.

And she grew . . .

...and
GREW.

Have you looked into a whale's EYE?

If you do, you'll see they know the SECRET of the Universe.